# THE GHOST
# WITH THE
# HALLOWEEN HIC CUPS

**By Stephen Mooser**

**Illustrated by
Tomie De Paola**

A Snuggle & Read Story Book

AN AVON CAMELOT BOOK

For Mom and Dad

2nd grade reading level has been determined by using the Fry Readability Scale.

AVON BOOKS
A division of
The Hearst Corporation
1790 Broadway
New York, New York 10019

Text copyright © 1977 by Stephen Mooser
Illustrations copyright © 1977 by Tomie de Paola
Published by arrangement with Franklin Watts, Inc.
Library of Congress Catalog Card Number: 77-6271
ISBN: 0-380-40287-4

First Camelot Printing, October, 1978

CAMELOT TRADEMARK REG. U.S. PAT. OFF.
AND IN OTHER COUNTRIES,
MARCA REGISTRADA, HECHO EN U.S.A.

Printed in the U.S.A.

BAN 10 9 8

Mr. Penny loved Halloween.

He was always in the Halloween play.

This year he was going to be the ghost.

On Halloween Mr. Penny
headed for town.

He met Bert and Laura along the way.

"Happy HICCUP Halloween."

"Oh my," said Laura.

"You have the hiccups."

"All HICCUP day," said Mr. Penny.

"That's too bad," said Bert.

"It's worse than HICCUP bad,"
said Mr. Penny.

"How can I play HICCUP a ghost
with hiccups?"

"What you need is a big drink of water,"
said Laura.

"Please, bring me some HICCUP water," said Mr. Penny. "The sooner I get rid of these hiccups, the HICCUP better."

Laura gave Mr. Penny a glass of water.
Then he held his breath and waited.
Ten seconds went by.
He didn't hiccup once.

"That did it!" he said. "My hiccups
are HIC CUP HIC CUP HIC CUP !"
Bert sighed. "I'm sorry," he said.
"Maybe you can get rid of them in town."

Mr. Penny hiccuped into town.

"Hello Ms. HICCUP Gates," said Mr. Penny.

"How are you HICCUP today?"

"I'm fine, but you sound terrible,"

said Ms. Gates.

"I HICCUP must get over the hiccups.

I have to be in HICCUP the play."

"Hiccups are easy to fix," said Ms. Gates.

"All you have to do is put a paper hat

on your head. Then you sing a song."

So Mr. Penny put a paper hat on his head.
He tried to sing, "Row, row HICCUP your
boat, gently down HICCUP the stream."
That was as far as he could get.

"Do you have any more ideas?"
asked Mr. Penny.
Ms. Gates was out of ideas.
But Mr. Brown thought he could help.
"Tickle his nose," he said.

Ms. Gates found a feather.

She tickled Mr. Penny's nose.

"HICCUP! AH-CHOO!" sneezed Mr. Penny.

"HICCUP! AH-CHOO! HICCUP!"

Mr. Penny started to cry.

"Now I have the AH-CHOO sneezes
as well as the HICCUP hiccups."

"What am I HIC CUP going to do?"
wondered Mr. Penny.
He went on down the road.
"The play starts HIC CUP in an hour."

Then Mr. Penny saw Mayor Bell.

"I have good news," said the mayor.

"Everyone is coming to the play."

"I have HICCUP bad news," said Mr. Penny.

"I can't be in the HICCUP play.

I have the HICCUP hiccups."

"But you have to be in it," said the mayor.

"Try hopping around on one foot," she said.

"Maybe you can shake those hiccups out."

Mr. Penny started to hop.

Every time he came down he hiccuped.

"Why don't you stand on your head?"
asked the policeman.
"I'll HIC CUP try it," said Mr. Penny.
"I'll do HIC CUP anything."

Mr. Penny stood on his head.

"This doesn't $_{HIC}C_{UP}$ work," he said.

"This just makes my $_{HIC}C_{UP}$ face red."

As it grew later Mr. Penny tried everything.
"Quack like a duck," said the butcher.
So Mr. Penny tried quacking like a duck.
But QUACK, HIC CUP, QUACK, HIC CUP,
QUACK was the best he could do.

"Try barking," said the dog catcher.
"I've never seen a dog with the hiccups."
"BARK, HICCUP, BARK, HICCUP, BARK,"
hiccuped Mr. Penny.

Mr. Penny shook his head sadly.

Mr. Penny went to a corner of the park.

He put a paper hat on his head.

Then he stood on his head.

"I'll give it one HICCUP last try," he said.

"One of the HICCUP things should work.

QUACK, HICCUP, BARK, HICCUP,

QUACK, HICCUP, BARK, HICCUP!"

The town clock said seven.

"I'll have to HIC CUP tell everyone
to go HIC CUP home," he said.
"I'm afraid they will be HIC CUP mad."

He crossed Mill Road. Then Mr. Penny
stopped. His hair stood on end.
It was a hairy bat and a dragon.

"HICCUP bats and HICCUP dragons!"
screamed Mr. Penny. "HICCUP help!"
He yelled, "run for your HICCUP lives."

The monsters ran after Mr. Penny.

"Help HICCUP, help HICCUP police," shouted Mr. Penny. He was so scared he jumped right out of his shoes.

"Please don't hurt me," he begged.

"Mr. Penny, it's only me," said the bat,
taking off her mask.

"And me," said the dragon. "We just
wanted to trick you for Halloween."

Mr. Penny sighed and shook his head.
"It's just that I was so upset by my hiccups
that . . ." Suddenly, Mr. Penny stopped.

"My hiccups are gone! You scared them
out of me. Now I can be in the play,"
smiled Mr. Penny. "Your trick has
turned out to be a Halloween treat."

And Mr. Penny was the best ghost ever.